Lion Island

ALSO BY MARGARITA ENGLE

ENCHANTED AIR:
Two Cultures, Two Wings: A Memoir

SILVER PEOPLE:
Voices from the Panama Canal

THE LIGHTNING DREAMER:
Cuba's Greatest Abolitionist

THE WILD BOOK

HURRICANE DANCERS:
The First Caribbean Pirate Shipwreck

THE FIREFLY LETTERS:
A Suffragette's Journey to Cuba

TROPICAL SECRETS:
Holocaust Refugees in Cuba

THE SURRENDER TREE:
Poems of Cuba's Struggle for Freedom

THE POET SLAVE OF CUBA:
A Biography of Juan Francisco Manzano

MARGARITA ENGLE

Lion Island

CUBA'S WARRIOR
OF WORDS

ATHENEUM BOOKS FOR YOUNG READERS

New York   London   Toronto   Sydney   New Delhi

A
atheneum

ATHENEUM BOOKS FOR YOUNG READERS
An imprint of Simon & Schuster Children's Publishing Division
1230 Avenue of the Americas, New York, New York 10020
ATHENEUM BOOKS FOR YOUNG READERS is a registered trademark of Simon & Schuster, Inc.
Atheneum logo is a trademark of Simon & Schuster, Inc.
For information about special discounts for bulk purchases, please contact Simon & Schuster Special Sales at 1-866-506-1949 or business@simonandschuster.com.
The Simon & Schuster Speakers Bureau can bring authors to your live event. For more information or to book an event, contact the Simon & Schuster Speakers Bureau at 1-866-248-3049 or visit our website at www.simonspeakers.com.
Book design by Debra Sfetsios-Conover and Irene Metaxatos
The text for this book is set in Simoncini Garamond Std.
Manufactured in the United States of America
0716 FFG
First Edition
10 9 8 7 6 5 4 3 2 1
Library of Congress Cataloging-in-Publication Data
Names: Engle, Margarita, author.
Title: Lion Island : Chinese Cuba's warrior of words / Margarita Engle.
Description: First edition. I New York : Atheneum Books for Young Readers, [2016]
Summary: A biographical novel about Antonio Chuffat, a Chinese-African-Cuban messenger boy in 1870s Cuba who became a translator and documented the freedom struggle of indentured Chinese laborers in his country. I Includes bibliographical references. Identifiers: LCCN 2015034288
ISBN 978-1-4814-6112-2 (hc)
ISBN 978-1-4814-6114-6 (eBook)
Subjects: LCSH: Chuffat Latour, Antonio, 1860—Childhood and youth—Juvenile fiction. I CYAC: Novels in verse. I Chuffat Latour, Antonio, 1860—Childhood and youth—Fiction. I Racially mixed people—Fiction. I Indentured servants—Fiction. I Slavery—Fiction. I Chinese—Cuba—Fiction. I Cuba—History—1810-1899—Fiction.
Classification: LCC PZ7.5.E54 Lio 2016 I DDC [Fic]—dc23
LC record available at http://lccn.loc.gov/2015034288

para mi amiga Celina
con su sangre de tres continentes
y dos islas

La libertad es la bestia que jamás
se amansa; rompe las cadenas que
le atan con sangre y fuego, para
recabar sus derechos.

Liberty is the beast that is never
tamed; it breaks the chains that
bind it with blood and fire, to
reclaim its rights.

—ANTONIO CHUFFAT

Contents

Historical Background

Beginning in the 1840s, more than 250,000 men were shipped to Cuba and Peru from China as part of a treaty between the Spanish and Chinese empires. Working in Cuba's sugarcane fields alongside African slaves, Chinese indentured laborers were often forced to sign one eight-year contract after another. Intermarriage between Chinese men and African women created a richly blended culture with unique religious, musical, and culinary traditions.

In 1868, a small group of planters in Cuba freed slaves and declared independence from Spain. Many Chinese Cubans joined the struggle for freedom, which turned into a series of three wars.

Around the same time, Chinese Americans were fleeing anti-Asian riots in California. By the early 1870s, five thousand refugees had settled in Cuba. Their experience with democracy and free labor inspired indentured workers. When China sent diplomats to investigate the treatment of laborers, personal testimonies suddenly offered an alternative to violence. Guns were no longer the only way to gain liberty. The power of written petitions offered hope. A Chinese African Cuban messenger boy named Antonio Chuffat documented the war of words.

Running with Words

ANTONIO CHUFFAT
Age 12

Year of the Goat
1871

Carrying Words

The arrival of *los californios*
changed everything.
School.
Work.
Hope.
All are mine, now that I have a job
delivering mysterious messages
for Señor Tung Kong Lam from Shanghai,
who fled to Cuba after only one year
in San Francisco.

California's violence must be dragon-fierce
to make so many refugees seek new homes
on this island
of war.

Shaped by Words

My ancestors were born
in Asia, Africa, and Europe,
but sometimes I feel like a bird
that has migrated across the vast ocean
to this one
small island,
as if I am
shrinking.

I don't know my *africana* mother's language.
I hardly even know her enslaved relatives.
I only know the *chino* half of my family.

Teachers call me a child of three worlds,
but I feel like a creature of three words:
Freedom.
Liberty.
Hope.

Craving Words

I was terrified when my father
brought me to this busy city of La Habana
from our quiet village.

He left me alone at a school
called *el Colegio para Desamparados
de la Raza de Color*—
the School for Unprotected Ones
of the Race of Color—
where I am only one of many
part-African children.

Most are orphans, abandoned, unwanted,
cast out like trash,
but I am here only because
my father wants me to learn proper Spanish
instead of blending it with his native language,
the Cantonese of southern China,
a huge country that I've never seen
and can barely imagine,
so accustomed am I
to this small island's
mixture
of thoughts
and tongues.

Lion Men, Peacock Men,
a Battle of Words

The messages I carry for Señor Lam
go to businessmen, diplomats, and soldiers
from two empires.

Spain's soldiers are familiar to me,
but until so recently, I lived in the little village
of Jovellanos, where I never saw imperial China's
regal visitors.

Military leaders from Peking wear sleek golden lions
embroidered on their chests like roaring hearts.

Soldiers of lower rank are marked by tigers, panthers,
or leopards.

But the most powerful symbols belong to diplomats—
men of words, whose silk robes are embroidered
with shimmering peacocks, long-legged storks,
or graceful
white herons.

Even a button can have meaning.
Red, pink, blue, clear crystal, brown clay.
Each hue grants a diplomat
the authority to settle
certain types
of arguments.

Whenever I hover in the corner of a fancy room,
awaiting a written reply that I can carry back
to my busy employer, I notice the way soldiers
always yield to civil officials.

These peacock-decorated peacemakers
are more respected
than growling-lion
military heroes.

Dream Words

When I close my eyes late at night
after school and work,
the comfort of sleep
does not
find me.

All I see is a dreamlike parade of beasts,
snarling and shrieking,
while dignified winged beings
quietly explain their POWERFUL
opinions.

Will anyone ever
listen
to me?

What would I say if they did?
Will I grow up to be a roaring lion-soldier
or a calmly speaking
diplomat-bird?

Weapon Words

POWER is a word that binds me in its spell
of fiery strength.

POWER allows Spain to rule Cuba.
POWER keeps *africano* slaves
and indentured *chinos*
in chains.

But I am free-born, working, studying,
and listening to Señor Lam
as he speaks of democracy. . . .

One man,
one vote!

Imagine having choices
instead of
FEARS.

Words Are Possibilities

During mornings at school, I recite Spanish
verb forms, but my afternoons are spent racing
with urgent notes written in Chinese characters.

Each message wrapped
in the warmth of my hand
feels alive.

Some are letters to the editors of newspapers
in Shanghai or Peking, and I am the one who runs
with feet that pound like drums
on slippery wooden walkways,
pummeled by rain that feels
like a hammer, driving ideas
into my mind.

Translation, understanding, an exchange
of meanings . . .
Could I ever be a patient diplomat, or would I prefer
the adventurous life of a lion?

Written Words

Señor Lam tells me that I would be
a good newspaper reporter,
the way I always
watch
listen,
learn,
before opening
my diary
to write.

Disturbing Words

Running, I pass slaves tied to whipping posts,
slaves chained to each other, slaves shackled
to wagons. . . .

Then I enter a neighborhood of *chinos*,
full of free men like my father, who completed
his eight-year contract, and refused to sign
another.

Who will speak up for the *africanos*
by writing letters to editors in Madrid?

Someday maybe I will, but for now
all I have is this job, carrying
words that will sail
to China.

Luxurious Words

At La Casa de Lam, some of the messages I carry
are letters to editors, but most are business deals
that result in shipments of jade, silk, porcelain,
lacquer-ware, furniture, medical herbs,
ivory figurines, sandalwood incense,
and other elegant
Shanghai treasures.

None of it is enough to make me value money
more than books.

At school, I study, then at work, I run,
and later, in my quiet room at night,
I write in my diary, remembering
every detail.

The Words of Emperors

When my father visits, I overhear his conversations
with Señor Lam, about injustice on this lion-fanged
island of brutal eight-year contracts.

The emperor signed a treaty with Spain,
agreeing to provide a quarter million workers,
ordinary farmers from Canton Province,
laborers for sugar plantations in Cuba and Peru.

As soon as the indentured men arrived on this island,
they were baptized and given Catholic saints' names,
during ceremonies spoken in Latin, a language
only priests understand.

The indenture system must end, my father insists.
Absolutely, Señor Lam agrees, as they go on and on,
speaking Cantonese, while I translate their words
in my mind, practicing Spanish so that someday
I can write letters to editors
in Madrid.

Warlike Words

The next day at school, instead of writing an essay
on ancient Greek philosophy, I hand my teacher
a page scrawled with rage.
Fierce words.
Ferocious words.
Words that stab, bite, scratch,
and threaten to burst into flames.
But my peaceful teacher smiles and says I'm learning
how to fight for my future, instead of battling
the past.

The Beast of Hope

Year of the Monkey
1872

Far From the Battlefields

Antonio

The freedom war began in 1868, a Year of the Dragon,
a time of hope, but now it just rages on and on
in distant mountains, while here in the city
my thoughts hover between peace
and rage.

Classmates leave school to rush off and fight.
Máximo Gómez, Antonio Maceo, Herculano Wong.
There are rebel generals of every race.
I could be one.

But my father wants me to obey his wishes.
Stay in school.
Study.
Work.

I'm accustomed to obedience.
So I wait.

Before a Feast
Antonio

When a wounded soldier passes me
on the street, I avoid meeting his gaze.

If we were on the same battlefield,
he would be my enemy.

Here in the city,
we are just neighbors.

A few minutes later, I watch Señor Lam's chef
as he chops ruffled cabbages, twining snake beans,
plump white radishes, and fragrant ginger.

It's the first time I've ever been invited
to eat a luxurious meal in my employer's
comfortable home.

Red lychees.
Golden melons.
Wine-hued passion fruit.
All these colorful foods are delivered
by a *californio* boy with a long braid
that shows his loyalty
to China's empire.

He stares at me.
I turn away.
I know what he's thinking.
My hair is short.
Curly.
African.
Different.

Places
Wing

The messenger boy is different, but so am I,
with a half-American mother who named me
for a soaring eagle, even though she knew
that the word should be pronounced Weng,
so that it would mean "glory" in Cantonese,
instead of "wing" in English.

Why think of her now?
Fever took her swiftly, while we were hiking
across the narrow bridge of jungled land
between North and South America.

Doesn't every refugee family
lose someone on that Panama trek?

Will this blaze of grief always burn
even more painfully than
fiery red peppers
on my tongue?

The Feast

Antonio

Forest-green cucumbers, olives, feathery herbs,
yuca, malanga, boniato, quimbombó, fufú,
ginger, five-spice, bamboo shoots,
all the foods of Spain, Cuba, Africa,
and China
mixed together
like music.

Señor Lam tells the vegetable vendor
how much he misses peaches, plums, pears,
and apples, northern fruits that refuse to grow
in tropical heat.

The same is true for spinach, celery,
and snow peas, Wing answers, crisp, cool vegetables
that his family grew and sold at their shop in Los Angeles,
town of angels, territory
of death.

La Reina de Los Angeles
Wing

The name of my hometown
clings to my tongue like mud,
reluctant to be spoken
out loud.

How dare Los Angeles call itself
Queen of the Angels?

Princess of Murder would be
more truthful.

After the Feast
Antonio

Wing's strange life story
floods into my ears
with the force
of a hurricane.

His speech is a rattling blend
of Spanish, English, and Cantonese.

How can so much suffering result
from attacks by men who believe in voting
and independence?

His home was a land of orchards
and gardens.

Now it is just a place of dust
and graves.

Memories of Murder
Wing

We lived on a rugged street
of sturdy adobe homes, shops, and corrals.

There were no Havana-style mansions,
no marble statues or luxurious fountains,
and no palm-thatched peasant huts
that will never
feel like real houses.

Summers were so dry in Los Angeles
that scant winter rain was stored in a pond.
We used it to irrigate thirsty fields and orchards
all year, making our Chinatown fruit shop
so valuable to our neighbors
that they called us the Miners
of Green Gold, even though
our fruit stand's true name
was Happiness to You.

We wrote every sign in three languages,
and Ba even learned a few native Kizh *indio* words,
so that all our customers would feel
welcomed.

Earthquakes.
Hot wind.
A season of dragon-hued fires.

Those were the only dangers we knew,
until drought made the cattlemen so angry
that they craved someone foreign
to blame.

No living member of my family has ever
been to China, but our eyes identify us
as descendants
of immigrants.

Rains failed.
Grass withered.
Cows died.

Empty pockets.
Empty hearts.

An ordinary fight about a woman
turned into a deadly brawl,
the rage spreading
like a wildfire
carried on the breath of a monstrous
smoky cloud.

By the time we realized that Chinatown
would be destroyed, it was too late.

Some of the sheriff's deputies tried to help,
and *mexicano* neighbors offered shelter,
but only women
and children
agreed
to hide.

I was a child.
My brother was older.
Jin and Ba walked out into the chaos
trying to bring calm, reasonable voices
into the swirling flames
of fury.
Ba survived.
Jin did not.

Death estimates ranged past two dozen,
all men and teenage boys,
hanged from fences
and oak trees
as revenge for
dusty weather,
mere dryness,
just a natural drought.

Warrior Thoughts
Antonio

If only I could roar
right out of my human skin,
and race all the way
across land and sea, to help Wing
seek vengeance.

No wonder all of Cuba's newspapers
call California a bloodstained Eden!

Señor Lam says those Los Angeles riots
were one of the largest mass lynchings
in United States history.
Only ten men were arrested, only four
were convicted,
and even they will soon be released.

No one in that nation ever pays for any crime
against people
who look different.

Almost Friends
Antonio

Sometimes I spot Wing in a crowd
of chefs and housewives, selling
his green gold from two enormous baskets
that dangle like portable gardens from the ends
of a thick, heavy pole that is balanced
across his shoulders
like the yoke of an ox.

Whenever I have time, I buy a snack of radishes
and stay to talk, but we are not quite friends yet.
Each of our words hangs in the air
like a test.

He asks about the scars on my face,
so I describe the wild Cuban herbs
used by Señor Doctor Kan Shi Kong,
who cured my smallpox.

Local News
Wing

No wonder so many islanders
keep asking me for medicines,
always quoting some saying
about *el médico chino*,
as if there were only
one Chinese doctor,
a magician
who can cure
any disease,
even smallpox.

The next time Antonio stops to chat, he brings
newspapers with articles about duels between
two reporters who fought with guns instead of words,
and a priest who was executed on a peaceful beach,
simply for blessing
a rebel flag.

There are quieter articles about masked balls,
church processions, charity banquets . . .
and a furious article about fistfights at banks,
where coins have suddenly been replaced by bills.

Paper money?
No wonder businessmen are furious!

Its value is less than half the worth
of precious metal.

What will I do if I can't earn enough silver
to help Ba buy the field he leases, so that we
can build a real house, with a tile roof
and a solid floor,
instead of palm thatch
and mud?

Evenings at Home
Wing

Muddy floor.
Palm-bark walls.
Flimsy, wasp-infested, vulnerable . . .
this thatched hut is no more protection
than a feather, when storm winds rage
and the island is buffeted by hurricanes.

Ba sits glum and silent, slurping the soup I've brewed
from whatever vegetables remained after I sold
all the others.

My twin sister hates cooking, so I do it for her,
happy to have some way to make up for my liberty
to roam as I buy fruit from other farmers, and re-sell
for a profit.

Fan can't lift the heavy baskets, so she's trapped
all day in the field with Ba, listening to his silence,
while she waits to grow up and feel free.

Stories
Antonio

I love to hear Wing's tales
about his twin sister's harmonious voice
and her odd name, Fan, a word chosen
by a part-American mother who liked it better
than the sound of "Fong," a real name
that means "bee."

Wing says Fan writes her own songs,
and re-invents others by changing
ancient Chinese poems.

Then he speaks of a makeshift altar
where his mother and brother are honored.

When it's my turn to answer questions, he listens
while I tell him about Cuban plantations, and the way
my father has figured out how to help runaway *chinos*
by inviting them to join paid *cuadrillas*—
salaried work gangs that are eagerly hired
during the frantic harvest season,
when every sugar planter
grows so desperate for laborers
that even Congolese slaves
and indentured *chinos*
are never
enough.

Plans

Wing

Antonio's description of free *cuadrillas*
keeps us both hopeful, as we speak of helping
just a few desperate people at a time,
but soon we switch back to war talk,
making plans for weapons and battles,
while we stand on a street corner, watching
pretty girls.

How easy it would be to join the rebels,
and yet how impossible
such a drastic change seems—
until I think of those riots
in Los Angeles, my brother, my town,
my real home. . . .

Then suddenly I'm so furious
that all I long for
is a chance to seek vengeance
against anyone
who is cruel.

Rage comes and goes in waves
like water, like storms.

My Father's Genius
Antonio

Free workers.
Wages.
Payment.
A contract for the whole free *cuadrilla*,
instead of each individual man.

No longer will laborers be locked up at night
or whipped, clamped in stocks, fed slave meals
of cornmeal and yams.

Rice, meat, fish, fresh vegetables,
all of this will be spelled out on paper,
and for once it will be the plantation owners
who have to sign contracts—which will only be legal
for a single harvest season,
not a lifetime of eight years,
and then eight more,
until old age, followed by
death.

The Underground Railroad
Wing

Islands have no borders,
just beaches.

Ships are the only way
to flee.

But Antonio seems so excited
about his father's free *cuadrillas*,
so I mention what I remember
from US history lessons
back when I was American,
and had time
for school.

Imagine
Antonio

Imagine a free territory
where slaves
could be hidden!

Imagine the difficulties,
dangers,
failures,
success,
satisfaction.

Imagine the POWER of helping
one helpless *africano*
or *chino*
at a time.

That Same Evening
Wing

With Antonio's dangerous vision
raging like a fire in my mind,
I walk away from the heart of the city
up a hill, toward the small plot of muddy land
where Ba and Fan have been hoeing stickery weeds
and planting tiny seeds
all day.

A sound.
A voice.
The dark road.
More voices.
Three Spanish soldiers,
in their fancy uniforms
with shiny medals, stopping me,
punching me, demanding coins,
metallic cash, not just the bank's
useless paper.

From a distance, the point of a bayonet
by daylight
looks no more threatening
than a mosquito, but up close
in star-shimmery darkness, it feels
like a flame.

So I give what I earned today,
along with a few onions and turnips
left over after a good day
of sales.

When the ordeal finally ends, and the soldiers
have moved on, I can't stop shaking
like a dry twig in a scorching Santa Ana wind.

I'm an immigrant, a refugee, a foreigner.
They could have asked for my papers,
the official *cédula*
that proves I have the right
to live in Cuba—the document
I left at home, in our hut, in order to keep it
clean and tidy, protected by lack of use,
just like my wasted, twisted fragments
of courage.

If Spanish soldiers ever rob me again,
I promise I'll fight back, join the rebels,
and overthrow
Spain.

Rage comes and goes in gusts,
like a hurricane's furious
wind.

Quietly, I return to work the next day,
trapped in the eye of my own
storm.

Assassinations
Antonio

What is the difference between execution
and murder?

Is it the age of a prisoner, his innocence,
or the seriousness of his crime?

These are the questions my teacher asks me
just a few days after Wing was robbed
and nearly killed.

These are the questions all my classmates
struggle to answer, without sounding like we're
daring to accuse the Spanish government.

Newspapers are filled with cautious reports.
Eight young Cuban medical students were just
shot by a firing squad.

Their only offense was scribbling insults
on the tomb of a Spanish reporter.
Now, other journalists are frightened.

But grown-ups are not as terrified as people the age
of that youngest student, the one who was only
sixteen. . . .

I'm thirteen.
Wing is fourteen.
Should we all be afraid
of being punished as traitors
if one of our whispered conversations
about rebellion is quietly
overheard?

When Words Travel Across the Sea
Antonio

Outraged by the execution of the medical students,
Señor Lam writes letters to the editors of newspapers
in China, while I scribble my own imaginary protests,
folding their non-existence
against my heart.

"¡Pobrecitos los cubanos!" Poor Cubans!
Those are the angry words my employer mutters
when he gives me a stack of sealed envelopes
for delivery to the post office.

The same words are written inside,
using elegant calligraphy, each line of ink
a work of art.

Imagine how far those words will have to travel,
bobbing and rocking on waves in a floating ship,
before Chinese officials will see them and decide
whether to care.

What good can it do, sending thoughts
to strangers?
Does Señor Lam
actually expect
educated peacock men
in Shanghai or Peking

to hear his complaints
about small
remote
Cuba?

Where is the POWER in words
that aren't heard?

Free
Songs

Year of the Rooster
1873

Beauty
Antonio

Finally meeting Wing's twin sister
is alarming and exhilarating.
I never knew that my mind
could be filled with a rush of feelings
instead of words.

Their family's leased farm is just a mud-hole
with rows of rice, shrubby things, and vines
that wrap themselves around other plants
like reaching arms with hand-shaped tendrils.

Wing is the one who cooks, while Fan serves.
We eat outdoors in the shade of a mango tree,
listening to the screech of green parrots
and the silence of Wing and Fan's grieving father.

Losing his wife during the crossing from California
to Cuba must have felt like torture
so soon after losing his oldest son
to the violence of rioters.

But once the sound of Fan's voice
reaches my ears, all I can hear
is beauty and hope.

Singing

Fan

There is no other way to help Ba
smile.

Only a song
can cheer him.

When words rise from my throat,
they feel like offerings
to heaven,
where Ma and Jin
must be singing too.

My Sister's Songs
Wing

She interrupted news that I wanted to hear.
Antonio was explaining Spain's troubles to Ba,
telling how King Amadeo just declared
that he is tired of trying to govern
a country he calls ungovernable.
He's abdicated the throne
and a republic has been established,
but of course it has challengers,
so in reality there's no government at all. . . .

And yet, despite that turmoil, Spain continues
to rule Cuba, and rebels in the mountains
still fight
for independence.

If my sister's voice did not shine with a magical
lightness of spirit, I would not keep listening
to her harmonious melody
and poetic words.

Mirror

Fan

Being the twin of a boy
is like shimmering
in and out of a shiny river,
the constant burst of rushing water
never peaceful enough to see my own
reflection.

Wing can go anywhere,
do anything, say whatever
he pleases, but I am a girl,
so I have to speak
cautiously,
work
endlessly,
and dream
only when I'm
singing
or asleep.

Shapes
Fan

Whenever I'm not in the vegetable field,
hoeing stubborn, thorny weeds with sullen Ba,
I practice all the gracefully painted characters
that I learned at our neighborhood school
in Los Angeles.

"Flame."
"Tree."
"Sun."
"Person."
Each Chinese character is a picture
born from the swoop of a brush, swish of bristles,
flow of ink.

But all I have is mud and a stick, so I scrape
the ancient characters that mean
"mouth"
"door"
"mountain"
"girl."

Lessons

Wing

Pond
in a bowl
reflected.

My sister carves fragments of verses
in mud or on stone, tree bark, a wall . . .
using our kitchen knife that is meant
for chopping onions.

Chinese characters, the English alphabet,
Spanish phrases, ancient poems and modern songs,
borrowed images mixed with her own, so many
sounds join to form
bittersweet music
like storm clouds
that hide the moon's
view of night.

Battle Thoughts
Fan

Twins tell each other everything.
When Wing whispers his angry plan
to run off and become a warrior,
I sing him an ancient Chinese song:
They dragged me off to war at fifteen,
and now I'm eighty years old,
finally traveling
home.

My brother does not want to hear wisdom.
He imagines that new violence can destroy
our old sorrows.

But Cuba's war for independence from Spain
has already gone on and on for long years,
and now even if the rebels win, there's no way
to be certain that all slaves—both lifelong
and eight-year—will ever be
set free.

Sky Thoughts
Fan

Where are you, Ma?
Can you and Jin hear my voice?
Do relatives in heaven see poems
written in mud?

When you were alive on earth,
you spoke of blue violets that your father
ate in China, to guide his meditation
on the movements of planets and stars.

Now I wish for those cool, silky petals
on my tongue, leading my mind
toward calmness.

Is it true that you greeted our twin births
with twice as many red eggs, and double
the mouthfuls of ginger?

Did you really call us animal nicknames
for one whole month, to fool
tricky ghosts?

You used to say that I was Squirrel
and Wing was Rabbit, but why didn't you choose
fierce names, to terrify
dangerous
spirits?

I could have been Panther, and Wing would be Lion.
Together, we would always be
fearless.

Ma, when fever defeated you, just before
we reached Cuba, did you really expect us to be
happy and safe here, instead of exhausted
and frightened?

The last thing you said to me was *fight*,
but did you mean that I should battle sadness,
or struggle—like Wing—against rage?

Mud Thoughts
Fan

This morning, a neighboring farmer
noticed the songs I leave written
at the edge of our field, and because
he cannot read Chinese characters,
he assumed that the shapes
must be evil.

He accused me
of witchcraft.

"Scapegoat."
I remember the English word so well,
from the riots, when our neighbors
suddenly decided that we were
strangers.

They stole your jade necklace, Ma,
the one Ba gave you as a marriage gift,
symbol of loyalty.

Then, because you were only half Chinese,
and the rest of you was mixed-together
British-German-French-American—
all those ordinary people
who used to be our friends
suddenly found chaos

an excuse
to treat us
like monsters.

But I won't let this new neighbor
imagine that I'm dangerous.

I talk to him in Spanish, explaining
Chinese characters, describing my purpose
as a songwriter, then calming his fear
with my voice.

Name Thoughts
Fan

Ma, on this island we were baptized
and given saints' names, but we choose
to ignore them.

Wing and I both prefer the two-meaning names
you gave to us, Wing for our birdlike hopes
and Fan to cool
our anger.

These not-quite-Cantonese
but not truly English
double-meaning names
are the only possessions
we still own
that ever belonged
to you.

Tree Thoughts

Fan

Wing leaves the hut with his baskets
each morning.

I try and try to lift them, but never manage
to succeed, so Ba won't let me be the one
to make a long trek into the city.

I'm left behind with his silence,
sharing the exhaustion of field work
and blunt tools
mosquitoes
ticks. . . .

Each verse I scrape into living wood
feels like a bleeding wound on my own skin,
but the sap that oozes from mango branches
is filled
with flowing dreams
of growth.

Air Thoughts
Fan

When I sing
out in the fields
at the top of my voice,
I feel like a windblown seabird
who has lost her migration path
and will have to wander forever,
or choose any tiny island
and build a new
nest.

Roof Thoughts

Fan

I invent my own character for "roof"
a delicate feather atop a sturdy house.
The feather is either landing or floating upward
toward sunlight—only the reader's mind
can decide which direction of movement
the curious eye detects—a tumbling
fall
or the flight
up to heaven.

In California, our roof was solid,
but here, the flimsy thatch rustles and whips
in storm winds, as if the first real hurricane
might suddenly whisk us away.

But what can we do to protect ourselves?
Nothing, so we sleep, and in the morning I write
new dream-songs
in mud.

Wife Thoughts
Fan

One day, an old African *babalao*—
a sort of priest—steps close to see
what I am writing on the ground.

He offers to tell my fortune in the pattern
made by tossing seashells and watching
how they land.

I thank him, but then I refuse, because what use
do I have for
a future?

Soon enough, Ba will marry me off
to the first old man who offers a bride price
of farmland.

Each time I bend to yank a weed from its place
in wet soil, I think of my own hopes, so rootless
and detached.

Independent Thoughts

Fan

Sometimes I feel
like I could rise
and float
along the path
made by Wing
as he trudges
toward the city
with his green gold
and his boy-hope.

Every time an oxcart
filled with sugarcane
passes close to this field,
I wonder if I will ever be
brave enough
to follow.

Song Thoughts
Fan

Can I change my own life?
Not alone,
but I'm a twin.

Wing tells me the names
of newly arrived businessmen
from San Francisco, wealthy men
who have not yet been told
to change their names.
Li Weng.
Song Sen.
Lau Fu.

They plan to open Cuba's first *teatro chino*—
a theater with a stage where I might sing!
Puppeteers could pretend that my voice
emerges from carved wooden birds.

All my dreams of butterfly harps, moon guitars,
bamboo flutes, *guzheng* zithers,
clashing cymbals, booming drums,
and resounding gongs—all my musical fantasies
could be real. . . .

Masks.
Face paint.

Costumes.
Dance steps.
Will the new theater hire girls?
Do I stand a chance?

I think of all the Chinatown operas I've seen
at our little neighborhood theater in Los Angeles.
Pear gardens, peony blossoms,
armored warriors, a love-struck princess,
the possibilities in a musical story
are endless.

White-faced villains, red-robed heroes,
blue for loyalty, pink for humor—in daydreams
I see myself singing behind masks
of every color,
so many meanings
as I sing from the depths
of a hollow wooden stage,
while above me, visible to all,
actors dressed as dancing birds
claim my voice,
my words.

On the Night Before I Run Away

Fan

I chop
feathery
wild fennel,
stir garlic
into soup
in a kettle,
toss in a few
woody
cinnamon
twigs,
and inhale
the spicy aroma
of my rapidly growing
boldness.

The Shadow Path

Year of the Rooster
1873

Musical Life
Antonio

Fan was hired by *el teatro chino*
as soon as she arrived, and now
her nightingale voice draws crowds
of admirers.

Later, backstage, she admits
that she misses the farm, with her freedom
to write in mud or on trees, sleeping in a hut
in the countryside, surrounded
by the music of nature.

Now, perched onstage, she wears
a feathered headdress, and sings of feeling
like the golden phoenix, a bird that lives forever
in legends, no matter how many centuries
of suffering
pass.

Public Life
Wing

What would Ba think if he came to the city
and saw his daughter singing in public
for so many lonely people
of all sorts?

I don't find her behavior shameful.
In fact, I feel so proud that I hesitate to share
what I know and risk having her image of courage
ruined by his criticism, so each evening when I return
to the farm with empty baskets and a full wallet,
and he asks if I've seen my twin, I reply
with lies about a respectable job
as a governess in the home
of a diplomat and his elegant wife,
where Fan does nothing more unusual
than teach children
how to write, sing, and play
traditional instruments.

My Lion Life

Antonio

I feel dangerous.
I'll battle any man who calls her
insulting names.

Cuban women in the audience
can be cruel, shouting their distaste
for unfamiliar Chinese melodies.

I'll protect Fan even more fiercely
than her own ferocious guard dog,
and that old woman with tiny, bound feet
who hovers backstage, ready to pamper Fan
just because she's famous.

The dog does not trust me, and the old woman
hates me, but I don't want their affection.
All I need is Fan's voice, singing
her hopeful poetry.

My Wish Life
Fan

Will you ever forgive me
for leaving Ba alone in the fields, Ma?

Can you understand how hard it was
to listen all day to that silent sorrow?

When I'm rich, I'll be able to help him
buy a house with many fields, hire workers,
build a shop, offer all the comforts
of California . . .
except for Jin
and you.

My Confusing Life
Antonio

Fan won't accept anything from me,
not even the jade necklace meant
for a future wife, or the poems I try
and fail
to scribble
in her honor.

At least she likes my name for her guard dog:
Moon, in her native English, because his face
is so round and gold, the glaring eyes
as big and dark
as craters.

Why does the soothing sound of each song
Fan sings
in this shadowy place
leave me feeling as lonely
as starlight?

My Masked Life
Fan

When I wear the grin of a monkey
or the claws of a tiger-princess, I realize
how rapidly songs change on islands.
Never the same words twice, rarely
the same melody—and rhythms,
the infinite drums, are all constantly
altered.

What is it about an island that makes everything
tumble, flow, and roll like rushing, roaring,
rippling
water?

I love the way an enormous variety
of dazzling Chinese instruments
gets all mixed up with Taíno Indian *maracas*,
African finger pianos, and Spanish guitars.

Why not?
This theater is big enough to offer
traditional Chinese opera on certain nights,
and inventive blends of mixed styles
on other nights, so that everyone
is eager to attend, even the complainers
who call my songs
too unusual.

Cuban music is like Antonio Chuffat's
altered surname, something ordinary
like the syllables "Chu Fat"—borrowed
and fused to form sounds that are new
and confusing, but intriguing
at the same time.

My Shadowy Life
Antonio

This theater contains so many
dark corners.

I feel like I'm haunting
the audience.

But all I want is time spent
listening.

School.
Work.
Hope.
All seem to fade as I waste my wishes
on Fan, whose voice sounds
like sunlight.

My Runaway Mind
Antonio

When my father visits,
he scolds me for letting my studies
grow vague and listless.

He scolds me for keeping Señor Lam
waiting, while I sneak into the theater
to gaze, and daydream.

He tells me to think of some way
to wake up from the haze of wishing.

So I do.
But not until after he reminds me
about the most exciting aspect
of his free *cuadrillas*.

Runaways.
Fugitives.
Eight-year indentured servants
whose tricky contracts
have proved unjust.

My father hides so many men in plain sight,
just by letting them work with the freed men,
pretending that they possess legal papers.

I don't ask about false documents,
bribed foremen, lies told to sugar planters
or corrupt officials.

All I ask is whether my father thinks the inside
of a hollow stage
would work as a hiding place.

Or would costume closets
be better?

Or the puppet workshop,
where a *californio* named Choy Men
carves sculptural
masterpieces?

A Useful Life
Fan

Finally, here is a future that makes sense,
an action I can take without leaving my place
backstage, after hours, late at night,
when the old woman sleeps,
and faithful Moon obeys me
in exchange for treats.

Yes, Ma, it's true, I'm a criminal now,
breaking unjust laws, helping
the helpless, hiding
escaped slaves.

Wing's tales of an underground railroad
in the US
entered Antonio's ears, and grew
like music, rising and spreading,
until I
was invited to participate.
Yes. That was my answer, Ma. I said yes.

I will help one runaway at a time
find a safe place to hide
in quiet
shadows.

A Life of Action
Wing

I know that protesting one injustice
won't change another one that happened
far away, longer and longer ago each day,
but at least it takes courage,
the most satisfying form
of my wavelike
comes-and-goes
storm-rage.

Knowing that we can do something real
instead of just dreaming—it helps me,
not just the runaways.

Fighting this war of shadows
feels as fierce as a real plunge
into the sort of war with sharp-bladed
shiny metal
weapons.

A Life of Limits
Antonio

Some feelings
are too vast
deep
turbulent
for these tiny
tidy
shapes
called
words.

What about the *africanos*,
my mother's people, lifelong slaves
not just eight-year servants—but where
can we hide them?
Certainly not here
where only *chinos* will become invisible
in a crowd of puppeteers
and musicians.

Terrified
Wing

On the day when the first runaway
is expected to arrive, all three of us
are so nervous that we forget
how truly frightened
the lone fugitive
must be.

My job will be feeding him from my baskets.
Antonio will usher him from this hiding place
to the next stop on an eerie shadow path.

Fan's only contribution to our scheme
will be her valuable silence, her ability
to keep a secret by quieting
her guard dog.

Courage

Fan

When I think of the punishment
for hiding runaways, waiting
for the first needy fugitive begins to feel
as dangerous as crossing that jungle of fevers
where you died, Ma—or returning
to the murderous flames
and ropes
of the riots.

So I sing to calm myself, I sing
to encourage myself, I sing
to help the others forget
reality
and risk.

Can a voice be used up?
Will I run out of words?
Am I like a paper lantern, burning?

Celebrations
Fan

No fugitive arrives.
Not today.
Not tonight.

Antonio says his father warned him
to wait for a festival, so that policemen
and soldiers would be drunk, and the streets
would be filled with distractions—dancers,
parades, and ordinary
fistfights.

So we wait.
In May, there is a *fiesta* to honor Guan Gong—
China's god of war and poetry, now transformed
into San Kuan Kong, which in the mouths
of Cubans quickly becomes Sanfancón,
this changeable island's patron saint
of runaways, both *africano* slaves
and indentured *chinos*.

My brother and Antonio speak
of possibilities, but in the end
they listen to me, and all three of us
end up agreeing that a feast day
that honors escapees
is too obvious.

 88

So we wait for June, the end of the sugar harvest,
when free *cuadrillas* are rich, and Antonio's father
is able to help by contributing money
for bribes.

Sea captains.
Sailors.
False document vendors.
So many details must be considered!
How will we decide which ships
to approach?

All we know is that the midnight chaos
during *carnaval* will offer the cover
of wildly dancing crowds
where anyone
can hide
just by swaying
and twirling.

The First Fugitive
Antonio

My father delivers him to an alley
behind the theater.
He's older, but still a boy, mixed race
like I am, with curly hair and startling
green eyes, but still *chino* enough in his appearance
to be mistaken for one of Fan's assistants.

This moment feels like my whole life's
great purpose—helping a runaway,
changing a hopeless man's future
simply with a mixture of dangerous action
and comforting words,
as I tell him
not to worry,
we won't betray him,
we'll make sure he's safe here.
Does he wonder, as I do, whether any of us
will ever be able to help our *africano* relatives,
whose form of slavery is so much more severe?

Two Wishes
Wing

We prepare as if this were still the *fiesta*
of Sanfancón, a dance that serves as a prayer
for runaways.

Fan tosses red and yellow ribbons
all over the theater, decorated with messages:
Share rice with the hungry.
Choose kindness and loyalty.

I've never understood how saints can represent
both peaceful poetry and fierce battles, but it fits
the double nature of islands, part fertile land,
part deadly sea.

When rage returns to my swaying-wave memory,
I still don't know which to choose,
the blood and flames of war,
or this slowly growing pathway
of shadows.

Love?
Fan

Meditate.
Contemplate.
Remember.
The messages on ribbons
mean that if you make a mistake,
it's hard to go back and start over,
but if love at first sight is an error,
then I will never try to correct
this moment.

The fugitive is familiar,
even though I have never seen him before.

I recognize his odd blend of bravery and fear.
It's the same as my own shy confidence
when I sing.

Perfect

Fan

Wing has cooked a filling dinner
of fried rice and banana fritters
for the runaway.

Antonio has found him false papers
and the uniform of a Boston sailor
headed to Hawaii.

When he tells us that his name is Perfecto SOA,
I'm baffled, until Antonio explains to me
the perplexing tradition of calling
babies with unknown fathers
SOA, meaning *sin otro apellido*—
No Other Surname.
Almost as if they don't
exist.

Hidden
Perfecto SOA

I was free-born, then trapped and forced
to sign an eight-year contract.

Antonio's father found me hiding in a forest,
and offered to help ship me far away across
the ocean.

I would have joined the rebels, if this chance
to sail away and forget my enslavement
had not presented itself
like a gift.

Mamá named me Perfecto because she
accepted me just as thoroughly as my father
rejected me, but she couldn't stop a priest
from writing "SOA."

Now I don't even know where she is anymore,
after so much moving from one sugar field
to another, slicing tough cane
with a machete, toppling plant stems
instead of cutting the cruel foremen
who wield nine-pronged whips
as if they are nearly complete extra sets
of human hands.

Helpless

Fan

With my voice wrapped
in unexpected emotions,
words from ancient poems
begin to flow anew,
joining
and twining
with my own verses.

Flood-dragon fury, a tired horse gazing
toward home . . .
Tu Fu's phrases lead me into a wilderness
of new words as I sing, imagining
a lost traveler,
searching.

I Almost Feel Like a Song Myself
Perfecto SOA

My weary mind
seems like a leaf
   swirling
in this wind
   of fortune,
past
and future
   equally
unknown,
   as my ears capture the girl's
perfect voice.

Perfect Craziness
Antonio

I've already known instant wishes
and then their loss, so I understand
the longing in Perfecto's eyes,
and Fan's, but there's no time
for love now, just common sense
and caution, because we have to
succeed in moving our first
rescued runaway
ever so swiftly
toward the harbor.

Maybe I really am more suited to calm,
orderly written forms of protest, instead of
all this fear transformed
into action.

Or is the combination
my natural talent?

Perfect Danger
Wing

Allowing the two of them to go on and on
whispering and singing as if this were a real
festival day, Antonio risks losing
any chance to reach
the foreign ship
on time
for tomorrow
morning's
early
departure.

A Life of Loss
Fan

Wing speaks.
Antonio listens.

Soldiers outside the theater.
Policemen on every corner.

Perfecto has to flee now,
before dawn brings the loss
of his chance.

Gone.
Vanished.
As if he'd never existed.

Ma, how does love survive
when the beloved becomes
distant?

More Songs
Fan

Less love, less life, less future,
more songs, more words,
more meanings.

Memory is such a mystery.
So much happiness
grief
rage
hope
all rolled into one,
like narrow messages
on a single ribbon,
carried away
by the invisible
sea breeze.

Dangerous
Flames

Year of the Rooster
1873

One at a Time
Antonio

After Perfecto SOA sails away
on a ship headed to Hawaii, I study,
work, daydream, and listen to Fan's songs.

So little hope of love
in my life.

Such a narrow
shadow path.

How discouraging it feels
to be able to hide
only one hopeful fugitive
at a time.

Many Fragments

Fan

We can't grow discouraged.
We have to keep trying!
Each runaway leaves us
with a few shards
of his broken
life story.

By the time we've listened
to all those tales of sorrow and wishing,
my own tiny world begins to feel
like a myth.

Still Grieving
Wing

I envy Antonio's school, his work,
the wholeness of his family,
and the way he always seems
to belong
on solid ground.

Without this pole and my two heavy baskets,
there would be nothing binding my feet
to earth, nothing but heavy waves
of ocean-wide
rage.

Poetry Is Dangerous

Fan

When I sing Li Po's ancient verses,
I feel as if I can really experience
the images from each poem.

He described throwing a mighty
mud-ball called Earth
into a sack, so that he could break free.

He spoke of dark battlefields
and men who swarmed like armies of ants.

Yes, I can see how the poems turned into protests,
while Li Po himself was foolishly drowning in a river,
after getting drunk and trying to embrace the moon's
reflection.

How can a hopeful poet ever know
what is true?

Flames of Bravery

Wing

Each runaway
who shivers
along the ghostly road
to freedom
leaves me
with the heat
of his burning
courage.

Flames of Confusion
Fan

Why did I fall in love with Perfecto?
Was it because he was the first
runaway
I ever met,
besides myself?

Instead of answers,
all I have is this endless smoke
from my blazing
questions.

Flames at the Harbor
Antonio

Vessels burn!
Ships catch fire,
and so do unloaded barrels and crates
on the docks, all Señor Lam's imported cargo
of finery. . . .

While Wing and I race back and forth
breathlessly carrying buckets
of seawater
to quench flames
on the boxes,
whole ships are already rising
and falling back into the sea
as wisps
of pale ash
floating.

Gunfire
Antonio

Were the fires set by rebels
or foreign invaders?

Troops patrol every street.
Students are interrogated.
School feels like a prison.

Classroom walls seem to be molded
of doubt, ceilings and floors
flooded by questions.

Newspapers call the dock fires
an accident, but those flames
were just the beginning. . . .

Now, all the whispered rumors
are about a ship
called the *Virginius*,
with an American crew,
captured by a Spanish war boat.
Reports say that most of the people on board
have been executed.

No trials.
No judges.
Just bullets.
Just death.

Uncertainty
Antonio

Newspapers call it the *Virginius* incident,
but wasn't it murder?

Señor Lam is afraid that the United States
will now attack Cuba, as revenge for the killing
of American sailors.

But were they spies, as Spain claims,
carrying ammunition to the rebels,
or was it just ordinary cargo,
food and clothing needed
for daily life?

Will our vast northern neighbor swoop
into our small island's war for independence,
making the mountain battles spread, grow, and last
forever?

A Fiery Future
Wing

Spain avoids vengeance by ending the crisis
with payments of coins for the relatives
of the American dead.

I feel so outraged by both the executions
and the settlement
that instead of rejoicing
along with Antonio, who believes in the power
of diplomacy, I begin to burn more and more
of my energy wondering
about war.

Solitude

Fan

Wing vanishes.
Then Antonio leaves too.

I'm left alone on our shadow path,
with no one but fierce, loyal Moon
to help me rescue desperate men.

A place to hide
is all I can offer.

No encouraging songs.
Just sorrowful ones, about the loss
of a twin's companionship,
amputation of half
my childhood's
hope.

The War Zone
Antonio

Right after Wing runs off to fight,
my father invites me to help diplomats
by listening to the stories of strangers.

I have no idea
what he means . . .
but I trust him, so I leave school,
abandon work, and forsake Fan,
leaving our shared
shadow plan
entirely
in her care.

Listeners

Year of the Dog
1874

Arrival
Antonio

Chin Lan Pin emerges from a regal ship
that represents the empire of China.

We meet him at the docks.
He looks like a king.
I feel like I'm inside
a storybook.

But all of this is real, every detail,
from the shimmering peacock feather
embroidered on his noble robes
to the smooth blue button and the red dot
on his gleaming silk hat.

As an imperial investigator, he moves
with the fearless confidence of a lion man,
even though his only weapons
are POWERFUL
words.

Petitions

Antonio

But how can my father and I be of help
when so many lion men, bird men, and servants
from both the Spanish and Chinese empires
suddenly bustle about, creating so much
polite, ceremonial chaos?

Spoken stories, Señor Lam explains,
will be recorded by scribes, who will write them
as official petitions for freedom
from the bizarre system
of eight-year-contract
slavery.

Many years of written pleas
from free men like Señor Lam
have caused distant ears to listen, and now
it is suddenly my turn to help anyone
who wants to tell his tale
to Chin Lan Pin.

My job is to roam
from farm to farm, speaking
to laborers, describing the process,
and inviting each man to participate
in the investigation.

Imagine the POWER of so many petitions.
Hundreds, perhaps thousands!

Already, I can picture brave stories
carried on ships, across ocean waves,
as the written words travel slowly
toward triumph.

Word Warriors
Antonio

Each man
who speaks to me
knows that the next time
he tells his story, the floating truth
will be written, so that it can reach
a palace in Peking.

Voices grow fangs.
Stories have claws.

Each of these weary laborers
is creating his only chance
to be free.

In the Land of the Lion Men
Antonio

As we ride through a dangerous war zone
escorted by the soldiers of two empires,
we pass prison camps where captive rebels
are punished.

I think of Wing, wondering if he ever reached
the mountains.

Was he caught along the way?
Is he one of the men in these camps,
chained,
enslaved?

Only three years ago, I was a child
fascinated by war stories.

Now I'm nearly grown, and my only dream
is peace.

Hungry Ghosts
Fan

For thirty days during the long festival
of ravenous spirits, hell-gates open
and hunger pours out.

Families feed eerie spirits with whole pigs, ducks,
and sweet oranges, as well as the ever-present
treasure of rice.

Wing waited so long for his chance to avenge
murdered relatives, but Ma and our brother
and the other hanged California men and boys
are still just as far out of reach as wandering spirits
from the *Virginius*, and those dead sailors
from the ship fires, and the eight medical students,
and all the ghostly soldiers, rebels, and villagers
from distant battles
in wild mountains.

Smoky incense.
Paper jewelry.
The offerings I make
before each performance
feel dreamlike.

I wonder if you can see me, Ma,
and hear my voice as I hurl

angry songs
up toward
heaven. . . .

If only I could visit you,
or fight the battle of truth
like Antonio, or join
the war of fire
and blood
with Wing.

If only I knew which form
of fierceness
can win.

My Ferocious Ears
Antonio

In windowless shacks, noisy sugar mills,
and steamy green fields, I meet eager men
ready to volunteer their voices.

My father lies to planters in Spanish,
then tells the truth to laborers
in Cantonese.

We pretend that we'll soon bring
more free *cuadrillas*, but in reality
we're simply here
to listen.

Word Rehearsals

Antonio

Each man speaks as if his life
depends on the strength
of his voice.
It does.

Each man speaks as if his secret words
are sacred.
They are.

Each man speaks in his own style,
crying out like a peacock,
or growling
like a beast.

So Many Ways of Speaking
Antonio

Some laborers describe harsh facts
as plainly as if they were doctors
or scientists.

Many argue like clever lawyers
in a courtroom.

Others recite as naturally as poets,
finally pouring all their slow years
of silence
into the swift
relief
of sound.

Pig Ships

José Chen

I was a farmer in Canton Province
when thugs kidnapped me and delivered me
to a Spanish doctor in Portuguese Macao.

I was forced to put my mark on a paper.
Strangers locked me in the depths of a vessel.
It was a boat designed for shipping livestock.

Trapped in the stench of that pig cage,
I shared the tiny space with hundreds of others
just like me, ordinary men suddenly cast down
into a seasick hell.

Now, each time I reach the end
of my eight-year contract, I am once again
forced to mark my *X*, so that I have already
chopped sugarcane in this strange land
for twenty years.

I Am a Man, Not a Contract

Francisco Wu

Eight years, then eight more, and now
on this island of laws and more laws,
I need only one of the following documents:
residence papers,
go-to-another-country papers,
open-a-store papers,
or begging papers.

In China, I was a doctor—so tell me, how
do I apply for a doctor's-license paper?

Am I a man, or a contract?
What sort of society decides
that special papers are needed
even by beggars?

Herded

Eugenio Liu

Wolves and tigers
would be less terrifying
than the whips and guns
of poison-heart men.

Snake minds.
That is how I think of the foremen
who guard us with weapons
while we live our ant lives.

Some of the foremen are Spanish,
but others are Chinese or African.
When it comes to cruelty, all nations
are equal.

Boiling

Juan SOA

Half *africano*, half *chino*, just like you,
who call yourself Antonio Chuffat.

Why should I believe you?

Do you really think I'll give you my true name,
when secrecy is my only protection?

Those of us who were born in halves
can be turned into eight-year slaves or lifelong.
It's the planter's choice.

Do you really think I'll be foolish enough to tell
a big peacock stranger from huge China
about my tiny-island life?

I would rather throw myself into a vat
of boiling cane, like one of those insects
attracted to sugar mill flames.
But I have no choice.

Your small, curled-up seashell ears
and the gaping monster-ears of Chin Lan Pin
are my only hope.

Take me to the peacock beast.
Let him listen.

My Ghost Story
Carlos Xu

Murdered in a forest.
I saw.
Who would speak?
I cannot.
So I live like an invisible spirit,
followed by shrieking crows
and howling wind,
knowing that I could be whipped
just like my friend, who bled to death
from many
narrow
wounds.

Look at these scars.

Yes, I saw the flight of my friend's soul,
but I am a silent witness—will the peacock man
see my marked skin, or close his bird eyes
in horror?

Arguing with Myself
Rafael Li

I possessed a freedom paper,
but on the second night of the fourth month
I was caught and enslaved.
My whole life was devoted
to helping my enemies
win a war that horrified me,
because I was forced to work
for Spain, instead of the rebels.

No wonder I keep trying to run away.
No wonder I continually
fail.

An Accidental Contract
Domingo Moreno

No soy chino—I'm not Chinese,
but I have just enough Taíno Indian blood
to make ignorant bullies see the hue
of my skin and the shape of my eyes
as an invitation to sign a tricky
eight-year contract.
I refused, so a foreman
signed the mark himself,
pretending the *X* was mine,
as if he found it impossible to believe
that I know how to write.

No soy chino. I'm not Chinese,
but after so many months in the fields
with eight-year slaves and lifelong ones,
I've learned quite a few words of Cantonese
and Congolese.

Will Chin Lan Pin hear my plea?

Wordless
Enrique Yi Tong

Loneliness is a land far beyond
the trembling borders
of language.

I arrived just last year,
so I don't know much Spanish.

When foremen with whips and guns shout,
their bellowing voices sound
like the smoke
of dragons.

Speaking for Many

Juan Chang Tai

From the pig ship
to a bird trap
fish net
squirrel snare
human cage.

Hear our petition.
Free us, along with
all our Yoruba wives
and their brothers,
our in-laws.

So Few Women

María Lu

We are only a sprinkle
in this rolling sea of kidnapped men
with new names, all of us baptized against
our will.

When I walk on an island beach, I see Kwan Yin,
the spirit of mercy who traveled along with me
all the way from home, just to accept
my quiet offerings
of fragrant jasmine
and salty tears.

Should I dare to take my petition
to an official?

When the peacock man listens,
will he wonder if I still feel
as beautiful as a vine
of wild jasmine?

In Between
Antonio

In the pauses between words, I hear
gasps, sobs, curses, and silent
prayers, so many ways
to wish.

Quiet Truths
Antonio

How difficult it is to describe injustice.
No wonder Fan used a knife on wood,
or a stick in mud, before discovering
her own songs.

What would Chin Lan Pin think
if he heard about those riots
in California?

There's nothing a warrior of words can do
for people who have already been murdered,
nothing but offer comfort so that the living
can begin to feel peaceful in the presence
of memories.

Such a Gentle Strength
Antonio

Soon all these hopeful tales
will be written and sent away
like feathery bird wings
that can travel
so much farther
than flaming claws
or bloody fangs.

Soon, my life
will make sense.

Stories, letters, translations.
Reports, articles, petitions.
These are the most POWERFUL ways
for me to help
slaves.

Voices
Heard Across
the Sea

Year of the Tiger
1878

Slow Decisions
Antonio

Years pass, more years, an agony
of waiting.

Soon after the imperial investigation,
ships delivering eight-year slaves from Shanghai
stopped arriving.

But more years passed, and the men and women
who had already signed tricky contracts
were still captives.

Now, finally—first in *La Gaceta de Madrid*,
then in *El Diario de la Marina*—bold reporters
publish a complicated two-empire declaration
that sets all indentured Chinese laborers
free.

When the Beast of Freedom Snarls

Fan

My songs praise the news, Ma,
but Antonio claims that the war
of words
is not over.

Between Triumphs
Antonio

Articles.
Letters to editors in Madrid.
Pleas sent all the way to Spain.
None of my efforts can rest
until the lifelong slavery
of my mother's people
also ends.

Men from Nigeria.
Women from the Congo.
Children of the Carabalí, Mandinga,
and every other tribe
deserve
liberty.

Between Battles
Wing

On my way to join the rebels,
I was captured by Spanish soldiers
and forced to work for the wrong army,
digging trenches, building forts, and cooking
for my enemy.

Eventually I escaped, and managed
to find the troops of Herculano Wong,
who welcomed me into a brave army
of Chinese Cuban warriors.

No traitors.
No deserters.
Not once did any of us fail
to fight courageously,
struggling to free
this little island from so many
enormous wrongs.

Now, the ten-year war is over,
and nothing was gained
but plans for the next war,
so I let myself return home,
enjoy peace, and rejoice

as I embrace my sister,
hoping my tired mind
and aching body
can finally
try to rest.

Celebration

Fan

Even though the rebels were defeated,
their families dance on Chinatown's streets,
acrobats leap, comedians twirl,
women weep, and my song
is just one
of so many
as men return
from battlefields!

Wing appears as if in a dream,
frowning instead of smiling,
even though later he admits
that he was daydreaming
as he walked,
imagining
a different life,
with you and Jin
still alive, Ma—a life
where we still own a Happiness shop,
although now our Chinese herbs
are mixed with island fruit. . . .

Black beans in a sauce
of tamarind and cardamom,
roast pork with mango
and five-spice,

guava dumplings,
seafood fried rice,
bitter melons
and sweet ones,
and always, strong *cubano* coffee,
side by side with Asia's tea.

Oro Verde—Green Gold—is the wistful name
of an imaginary restaurant in Wing's nostalgic
daydream, so I buy a building with my song money,
and we open during the quiet time between wars,
when nothing seems more powerful
than this mixture of old memories
and new hope.

Twins Again

Wing

Fan tells me that she visited Ba
while I was gone.

He has a new family:
a Spanish Congolese wife,
and a baby, our half sister.

When they come to the restaurant
smiling and laughing, I feel as if all of us
belong to some other life,
a world without any wars
sorrows
separation. . . .

Slow Voyages
Perfecto SOA

Just like the words that traveled
across oceans in the form of petitions,
I've journeyed from continent
to continent, visiting all the lands
of my many ancestors,
known
and unknown.

I've witnessed wonders
and horrors
in every nation.

Only one more journey now, this rush
from crowded docks to the theater, to see if Fan
remembers that moment when our eyes
first met,
and we knew
as if by magic
that our voices
belong together,
sending the shared
music of love
skyward,
like ribbons
in a sea breeze.

Carrying the Beast of Hope
Antonio

By the time Perfecto and Fan
are reunited, I no longer imagine
that she and I were ever meant
to be together, or that I might someday
become a gunfire warrior like Wing.

I have my own journeys now,
as a translator for China's consulate,
carrying messages for diplomats,
sailing across many oceans, delivering
possibilities for peace,
and writing, always writing,
trying to change the world around me
by hurling weapon-words
onto the POWER of paper that travels as lightly
as feathers, while words growl as fiercely
as fangs.

Historical Note

All the major events described in *Lion Island* are factual, but I have imagined numerous details. Antonio Chuffat, his father, Señor Lam, and Chin Lan Pin are historical figures. Wing, Fan, and Perfecto SOA are fictional characters, as are the various indentured laborers whose petitions are portrayed here.

According to Antonio Chuffat's unusual third-person memoir, theaters and free *cuadrillas* ("work gangs") really did serve as hiding places for runaway indentured laborers.

Testimonies in the section called "Listeners" are inspired by real pleas for freedom, presented during China's official investigation of abuses of the contract servitude system. Many of the original pleas were written in verse, in what may be one of the largest and most successful collections of petitions for liberty ever filed in any archive. Originally written in Chinese, most of the testimonies have not yet been translated into Spanish or English.

Five thousand Chinese Californians really did find refuge in Cuba after fleeing anti-Asian riots, including the October 1871 mass lynching in Los Angeles. The arrival of experienced businessmen from California inspired Chinese laborers on the island to hope for jobs outside the indenture system. Impressed by the confidence, skill, and democratic principles of the refugees, Chinese

Cubans in turn influenced *los californios*, who joined the complex, multifaceted struggle for independence from colonial rule, freedom from forced labor, and liberty of expression, both written and spoken.

Antonio Chuffat went on to become a champion of civil rights for the Chinese Cuban community. He traveled the world as a translator for Havana's Chinese consulate, and founded the island's first Chinese-language newspaper. After Cuba's third and final war for independence—known in the United States as the Spanish-American War—he spoke out against anti-Asian immigration policies imposed by US occupation of the island.

Chuffat said nothing about his African mother and her family in his memoir, which was presented as a study of Chinese Cuban history. However, in 1912, when former slaves rebelled against continued inequality in the post-emancipation era, Chuffat finally had his chance to become an outspoken champion of civil rights for the African Cuban community as well.

Lion Island is the final volume in my loosely linked group of historical verse novels about the struggle against forced labor in nineteenth-century Cuba. The other books are *The Poet Slave of Cuba: A Biography of Juan Francisco Manzano*; *The Surrender Tree: Poems of Cuba's Struggle for Freedom*; *The Firefly Letters: A Suffragette's Journey to Cuba*; and *The Lightning Dreamer: Cuba's Greatest Abolitionist*.

References

Chuffat Latour, Antonio. *Apunte histórico de los chinos en Cuba*. Habana: Molino y Cia, 1927.

Hinton, David, editor and translator. *Classical Chinese Poetry: An Anthology*. New York: Farrar, Straus and Giroux, 2008.

López, Kathleen. *Chinese Cubans: A Transnational History*. Chapel Hill: University of North Carolina Press, 2013.

Seuc, Napoleón. *La colonia china de Cuba, 1930–1960: Antecedentes, memorias y vivencias*. Miami: Napoleón Seuc, 1998.

Yun, Lisa. *The Coolie Speaks: Chinese Indentured Laborers and African Slaves in Cuba*. Philadelphia: Temple University Press, 2008.

Further Reading for Young People

To learn more about the history of Chinese Californians, read *The Golden Mountain Chronicles* by Laurence Yep. New York: Harper Collins (10 volumes, various years).

To learn more about Chinese music, read *Summoning the Phoenix* by Emily Jiang, illustrated by April Chu. New York: Lee & Low, 2013.

Acknowledgments

I thank God for the power of words.

As always, I am grateful to Curtis and the rest of our family for support and encouragement.

Special thanks to antiquarian booksellers Dan and Peggy Dunklee at A Book Barn in Clovis for helping me obtain my own treasured copy of Antonio Chuffat's extremely rare memoir.

Profound gratitude to Mary Wong, Phillip Wong, Jackie Wong, Janet Wong, Adriana Méndez, William Luis, Myra Garces-Bacsal, Kenneth Quek, and Joy Chu for making corrections. Any errors that remain are entirely mine.

Enthusiastic cheers for my wonderful editor, Reka Simonsen; my agent, Michelle Humphrey; artist Sean Qualls and designer Debra Sfetsios-Conover, for the beautiful cover; and the entire Atheneum publishing team!

The following resources were helpful:

FIU Cuban Research Institute

Smithsonian Latino Center

Chinese American Museum of Northern California

cubaheritage.org

yeefowmuseum.org

californiahistoricalsociety.org